For my baby girl, Amira Sanaa.
–M.C-G.

For all the kids in the pool pretending to be mermaids.
–M.O.

The Mermaid Princesses
Text copyright © 2020 Maya Cameron-Gordon
Illustrations copyright © 2023 Maya Cameron-Gordon
All rights reserved. Manufactured in Italy.
No part of this book may be used or reproduced in any manner whatsoever without written permission
except in the case of brief quotations embodied in critical articles and reviews. For information address
HarperCollins Children's Books, a division of HarperCollins Publishers, 195 Broadway, New York, NY 10007.
www.harpercollinschildrens.com

Library of Congress Control Number: 2022930100
ISBN 978-0-06-320525-3

The artist used Photoshop Creative Cloud to create the digital illustrations for this book.
Typography Elaine Lopez-Levine
22 23 24 25 26   RTLO   10 9 8 7 6 5 4 3 2 1
❖
First Revised Edition

THE MERMAID PRINCESSES

written by **MAYA CAMERON-GORDON**

illustrated by **MIRELLE ORTEGA**

HARPER
An Imprint of HarperCollinsPublishers

Deep beneath the sea, there lived three mermaid princesses.

ANAYA WAS THE KINDEST AND SWEETEST.

Whenever underwater creatures of the sea were sad
or scared, Anaya sang beautiful songs to soothe them.

SHANTE WAS THE STRONGEST AND BRAVEST.

For fun, she explored parts of the ocean
others would not dare to go.

KIANNA WAS THE WISEST AND LOVED TO LEARN.

She spent her days studying the different plants
of the sea and could identify any one of them.

Since they were teeny tiny, each of the sisters dreamed
of one day being queen.
It was the one thing they *definitely* had in common.

"When *I'm* queen, I will make every day a different holiday," Anaya declared.

"As queen, *I* am going to build a library filled with the oldest books from around the world," Kianna argued.

"Both of you are wrong! *I* will be queen and will explore every part of the sea as I build strong ties with merpersons everywhere!" Shante insisted.

The mermaids swam to the one merperson who knew everything about being queen.

They approached the throne and asked . . .

"MOMMA! MOMMA! MOMMA!

WHICH ONE OF US WILL BE QUEEN?!"

Before the queen could get a word out, the princesses
were bickering back and forth about who was a better fit.

"That's enough!" The queen ordered the mermaids out.
"*Whoever* is to be queen must first and foremost be
a good sister and protector."

"YES, MOMMA."

The princesses drifted away without
an answer to their question.

As they swam farther out beyond the palace,
they heard a whistling sound that grew

LOUDER
AND
LOUDER.

The sound led them to a dark cave, where they saw a baby dolphin stuck in a net.

"**OH NO!**" Anaya cried.

"We've got to do something!" said Shante as she pointed to a shark gliding toward the baby dolphin.

"I think I have an idea," said Kianna. She explained her expert plan to her sisters.

"**LET'S DO IT!**"

First, Anaya swam out from behind the rock and began to sing.
Hungry and frantic, the shark thrashed toward her.

Until suddenly, Anaya's song had taken effect.
The more Anaya sang, the calmer the shark became.

Shante bravely swam past the shark and approached the baby dolphin. It had been so frightened that it wiggled around, entangling itself in the net.

The knots were almost impossible to untangle. But when Shante saw the fear in the dolphin's bright blue eyes, she refused to give up.

She used all her strength to get it out, and, at last, the baby dolphin was free!

"Anaya, we never could have done this without your sweet voice," Kianna said.

Kianna turned to Shante. "Or without your courage."

"And we couldn't have done it without your clever plan, Kianna," her sisters replied.

The three sisters felt a warmth
fill a place in their hearts.

When the princesses entered the palace, they hugged their mama tight.

"We're sorry, Momma. We'll never fight about who will lead again."

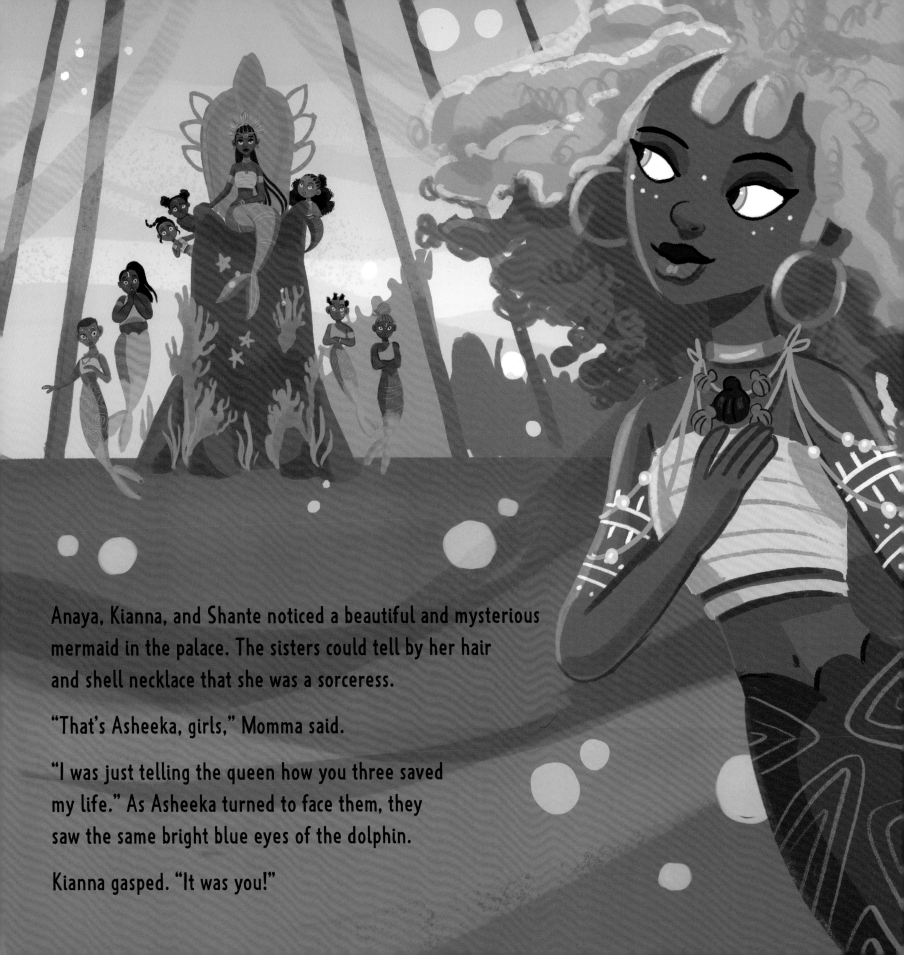

Anaya, Kianna, and Shante noticed a beautiful and mysterious mermaid in the palace. The sisters could tell by her hair and shell necklace that she was a sorceress.

"That's Asheeka, girls," Momma said.

"I was just telling the queen how you three saved my life." As Asheeka turned to face them, they saw the same bright blue eyes of the dolphin.

Kianna gasped. "It was you!"

The sorceress smiled. "That's right. And I have decided to return your kindness with a gift. You princesses have heavy hearts and are seeking answers about your future. I will allow you one question."

The three princesses had the same question:

"WHICH ONE OF US IS BEST SUITED TO BE QUEEN?"

Asheeka shook seashells in the palm of her hand and let them fall to the ocean's bottom. "The shells tell me that the ocean needs a queen that is as strong and fierce as a shark, as clever and wise as an octopus, and as kind and caring as a dolphin."

Word spread. Merfolk from across the ocean gathered to celebrate and bring the princesses gifts.

From that moment on, the mermaid sisters began their training to become queens—together . . .

and were well on their way to becoming **LEGENDS** of the sea.

THE END.

FUN FIN FACTS!

DID YOU KNOW? Mermaids have been a part of African culture for hundreds of years. In the part of Africa closest to the US (West Africa), there is an ancient myth about a mermaid named Mami Wata. Her name means "Mother Water."

WHAT DOES MAMI WATA LOOK LIKE? Half-human and half-fish!

DOES MAMI WATA HAVE SUPERPOWERS? Yes! She can heal people and make them rich. She can also charm snakes and sink ships! Mami Wata is both respected and feared!

DID YOU KNOW? There is an African mermaid named Yemaya who is said to be "the mother of all" and celebrated as a goddess (an Orisha)! She is known throughout African, Caribbean, and South American cultures!

DOES YEMAYA HAVE SUPERPOWERS? Yep! She is believed to bring love, life, and healing to anyone who believes in her.

WHAT DO PEOPLE DO TO GET BLESSINGS FROM YEMAYA? They bring her offerings, such as honey, watermelon, or white flowers.

DID YOU KNOW? In some areas of West Africa, it is believed people can use cowrie shells to see the future! How did they do it?

⭐ They set up a table or place a mat on the floor.
⭐ A priest or priestess sets down sixteen cowrie shells.
⭐ They make their requests to the Orishas.
⭐ The Orishas answer by making the shells fall a special way.
⭐ The priest or priestess reads the shells and lets the person know what the gods said.